# THE POINTED BRUSH

*by*

Patricia Miles Martin

*Illustrated by Roger Duvoisin*

Chung Yee, the smallest of six sons, was chosen to learn to read and write because he was too small for his father's rice fields. He was sad because his older brothers wanted to learn and Chung Yee knew of the power of the written word. Elder Uncle was accused of stealing a water buffalo and the older brothers were sent to get him out of the bamboo cage where he was confined in town. They returned with bruised heads, but without Elder Uncle. So the sixth son moistened his brush and wrote a letter. Look at the letter Small Sixth wrote (it looks very different from yours) and then see what happened when the villagers read it!

\* \* \*

Dewey Decimal Classification: F

## *About the Author:*

PATRICIA MILES MARTIN spent her childhood on her grandfather's Kansas farm, grew up in Denver, and taught school in Colorado. She now lives in California. She feels that boys and girls need to know *why* they must learn — at school, at home, everywhere. This book is to show them the power of the written word.

## *About the Illustrator:*

ROGER DUVOISIN was born in Switzerland and spent his childhood there and in France. His father was an architect. He studied art in Geneva, specializing in mural painting and stage scenery. He also worked with ceramics and textiles. In addition to the Caldecott Medal he won in 1948 for the illustrations in *White Snow, Bright Snow*, he has received many other awards, among them one from the government of West Germany for his illustrations for *The Happy Lion*, written by his wife, Louise Fatio.

# THE
# POINTED
# BRUSH

This edition lithographed in U. S. A. by Wetzel Bros., Inc., Milwaukee 2, Wisconsin

# THE POINTED BRUSH

BY PATRICIA MILES MARTIN

ILLUSTRATED BY
**ROGER DUVOISIN**

1964 FIRST CADMUS EDITION
THIS SPECIAL EDITION IS PUBLISHED BY ARRANGEMENT WITH
THE PUBLISHERS OF THE REGULAR EDITION
LOTHROP, LEE & SHEPARD CO., INC.
BY
**E. M. HALE AND COMPANY**
EAU CLAIRE, WISCONSIN

Chung Yee, who was only the small sixth son in the house of Chung, trudged down the path toward his home, carrying a little box of dried ink and a long brush. His steps were slow, for Chung Yee was sad.

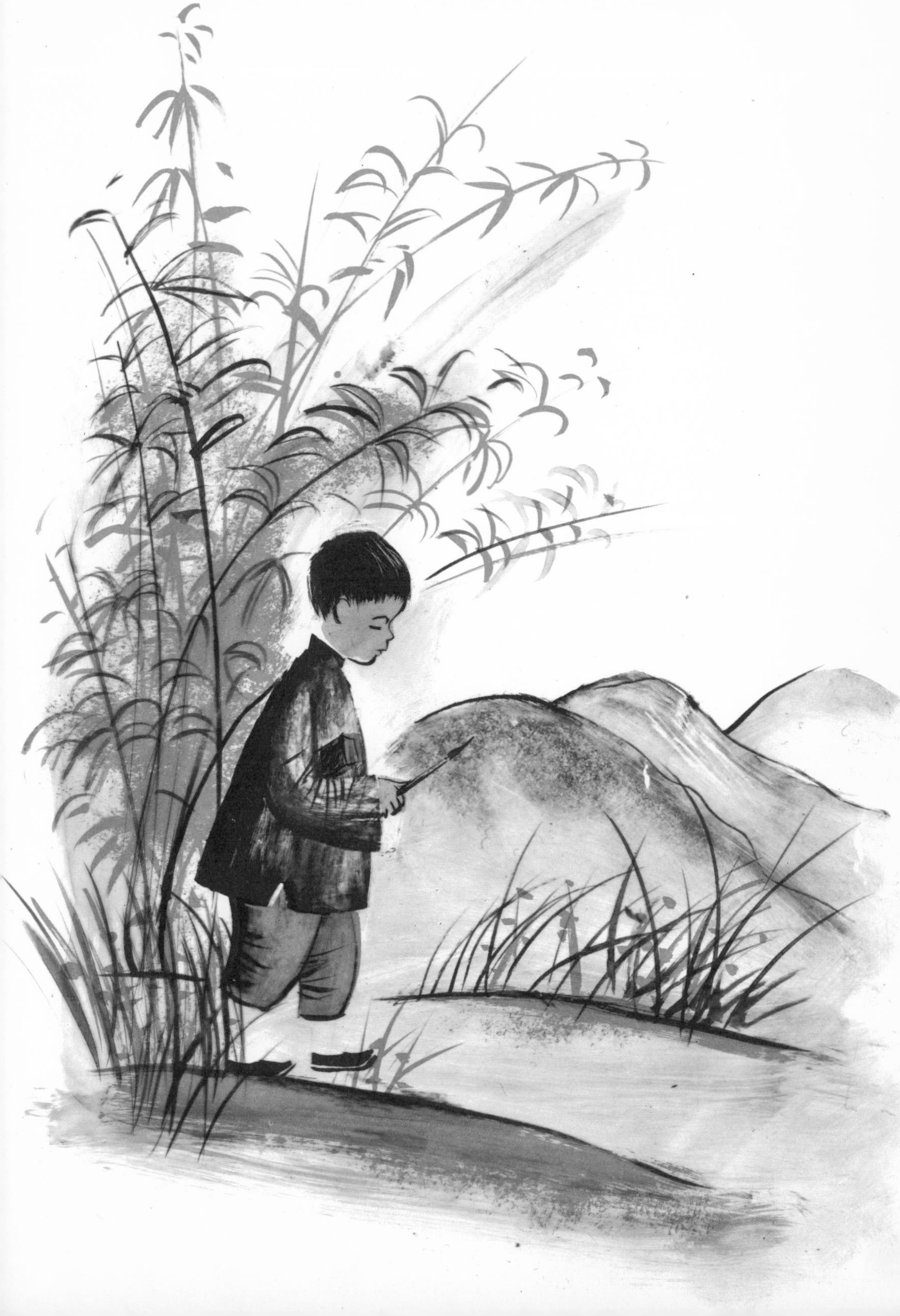

He heard the booming voice of Elder Uncle.

"Ho, Small Sixth! Wait for me! I go to spend the night at your house. Wait for me. Let us walk together."

Chung Yee turned and waited respectfully at the side of the path, with his hands folded over his wide sleeves.

"You look sad, Small Sixth," Elder Uncle said. "Is there sorrow in the house?"

"That is so." Chung Yee bowed. "I am sad because my brothers wish to learn to read and to write. My mother has begged our father to allow all of us to sit at the feet of the teacher. But I am the only one chosen."

"And why are you so favored?" Elder Uncle looked down at Chung Yee.

"I am the youngest and the least needed in the rice fields."

Elder Uncle nodded. "I see."

"My teacher has taught that there is power in the written word, and because my father wishes his sons to be powerful, I have told him of the power in the written word," Chung Yee said.

"And what did my Honored Brother-in-law say to that?" Elder Uncle asked.

"He did not agree," Chung Yee replied.

In silence they walked on in the cool of the late afternoon, until they came to a rice field where Ling Po, a farmer, was working. He stood ankle deep in water and he slapped at his water buffalo and shouted in high pitched tones.

"Yi! You turnip! Turn, Pig-headed One!"

"Good evening, Old Farmer," Elder Uncle called politely. "You have a handsome water buffalo there. A strong, well-built animal. Notched in the right ear, I see."

The farmer stopped and pushed his hat back on his head but did not reply. He seemed of slow wit.

"A fine buffalo!" continued the Uncle. "You are fortunate to have such a splendid creature. I only wish that I had an animal half so good."

As they walked on, the first star of night came out. "I shall be glad to sleep in the peaceful house of my brother-in-law," Elder Uncle said. "My day has been filled with haggling in the market place."

That night when Chung Yee looked at Old Chang, the man in the moon, his mother murmured, "Old Chang will give you sweet dreams, my son."

The next morning after a good night's rest, Small Sixth roused Elder Uncle. His mother lighted the charcoal brazier and put on water for the rice. She served tea in small cups without handles and Chung Yee held the cup in both hands to warm his fingers.

When the rice bowls were filled, there was a great shouting outside and a loud hammering on the door.

Chung Yee's mother ran to open the door, but it was flung rudely wide, before she reached it.

Ling Po the Farmer stood there, flanked on each side by a soldier. He pointed to Elder Uncle.

"This one is the man," he said.

The soldiers stepped forward. "Come." The voice of the soldier was rough as the rasp of a hand saw, and he prodded Elder Uncle with the barrel of his gun.

Elder Uncle rose quickly, spilling his rice in his haste. Small Sixth felt the flutter of butterflies in his stomach.

"What have I done?" Elder Uncle cried out, and answered himself, protesting. "I have done nothing! Nothing!"

"Come," the soldier said. "Move!"

The old farmer stood looking from one face to another. "He has stolen my water buffalo," he chanted. "He has stolen my water buffalo."

"I am an innocent man!" Elder Uncle cried for all to hear. But the soldiers led him away.

Now Chung Yee knew that his uncle did not steal the buffalo, but he did not know what he might do to help. He listened to the wail of his mother as she hugged herself and rocked back and forth.

His father stroked his thin beard and said, "Do not weep, Wife. Elder Uncle is innocent. I will have him here before the moon sails in the sky tonight. I have strong sons who will bring him home."

He turned to his eldest son.

"First son," he said, "your muscles are the muscles of a man. Your strength is the strength of two men. Your courage is the courage of three. Follow the soldiers to the village. Watch at a distance while they lock Elder Uncle in the bamboo cage. You understand?"

"I understand." The eldest son nodded his head.

"Now," his father said, "when the soldiers have left the cage, you wrench apart the bamboo stakes that confine our uncle and bring him back."

The first son ran down the path toward the village.

Small Sixth sat on his heels and thought about Elder Uncle. He thought about the Head Man in the town and the scholars who gathered at the teahouse there.

Now, some time later, the first son returned from the village with a bump on his head the size of an egg and a bruise over one eye as black as ink.

He bowed to his family. "The soldiers assailed me. It is not enough that I have the strength of two men. It is not even enough that I have the courage of three."

Beyond the town, a water buffalo with a notched ear wandered free, and he trailed a broken thong.

The father turned to his second son. "Go to the village," he said, tugging at the few long hairs of his beard. "Find the bamboo cage where Elder Uncle is confined. When the soldiers turn their backs, wrench apart the bamboo stakes and free Elder Uncle."

He turned to his third, fourth and fifth sons. "You three," he said, "you will follow Second Son. If the soldiers molest him when he frees Elder Uncle, you will attack as do the grasshoppers in the cabbage crop. Bring back Elder Uncle."

Later the four sons returned. The second son had a
bump on his head as large as two eggs. The third son had
a bruise and it was blue and yellow and purple as the
water colors in a paint box, and the fourth and fifth sons
were limping and groaning.

The second son bowed. "You can see for yourself,
Honored Father, we have been beaten with sticks. We
could not rescue our uncle."

Beyond the town a water buffalo with a notched ear trailed a broken tether, and wandered toward the bridge that crossed the moat.

Small Sixth rose from his heels and took his box of ink from a low table. He spread a piece of rice paper on the floor before him and picked up his brush.

He pointed it carefully with his lips.

He laid the pointed brush across the dried ink and he wrote in long lines.

*"Honored and Respected Elders:*

    *I am the sixth son of Chung Kan. I write you of Elder Uncle who is held in a bamboo cage in the village. My revered Uncle is accused of the theft of a water buffalo belonging to Ling Po, the Farmer. May I ask your help?*

    *First, may I ask that you help to restore Our Uncle to his family. You all know the good reputation of my Honored Uncle. You know that he is an innocent man, accused in error and held by force.*

    *Second, may I ask your help in finding the water buffalo for the Old Farmer? The water buffalo is a fine animal of great strength, and his right ear is notched."*

Again, the sixth son moistened the brush and pointed it with his lips. He signed the letter boldly. When the ink was dried, he rolled the rice paper and tucked it in his sleeve. While his father comforted his weeping mother, Chung Yee ran down the path toward the village.

諸位大人鈞鑒 小子乃鍾幹之第六子

因伯父被錮於本村之竹籠中並被

控偷竊農民凌寶之水牛有所

懇請者竊查（伯父之聲譽量為

大人等所深知此次被控盜竊實

屬無罪敬請

大人等設法將彼釋放再者該農民

之水牛強壯力大右耳有切痕亦懇

大人等代為設法尋找為禱

敬請

均安

愚第鍾籛升頓

THE LETTER OF SMALL SIXTH

When he reached the teahouse, he fastened the notice to the outside wall, and waited there in the garden beneath a plum tree.

The scholars of the village read the notice and murmured among themselves.

"We will notify all the villagers of this injustice," they said. And Chung Yee watched while they went their different ways.

Before long, people gathered in a great crowd and pushed through the moon gate that led to the Magistrate's garden.

Chung Yee sat waiting. He felt a shadow cross his face. He raised his eyes to see his father standing before him.

"My son, why are you here?" His father frowned.

"I have posted a letter about Elder Uncle to test the power of the written word, Honored Father."

"Is this the letter?" Chung Kan pointed a long finger.

"Yes, Father," the sixth son replied.

Chung Kan ripped it from the wall. "Foolish one," he said, "it is unwise to act without permission." He tore the rice paper across. "You are to be punished. You will no longer go to the teacher. You will remain home with your brothers and work in the rice fields."

Chung Yee did not speak. He looked down at his own feet, and he followed his father out of the town

over the bridge and across the moat, toward home.

There, around the charcoal brazier, the family sat si-
lently, waiting for the water to boil for tea.

Suddenly, they heard laughter and Elder Uncle's tall
figure filled the doorway.

"I am freed!" he said. "The people of the village spoke for me! They went to the Magistrate and demanded my freedom. I am a man of fine reputation and I was freed!"

Chung Yee's father sat silent.

After a moment, he clapped his hands. "My sixth son has proven himself more powerful than his brothers," he said. "The teacher is right. The man who knows the written word has strength."

His mother poured a cup of tea and handed it to Chung Yee's father with trembling fingers.

The father spoke again. "I want no weaklings in my house. All of our sons shall go to the teacher. They shall grow wise, knowing the written word. They shall grow powerful."

"But who will tend the rice fields, Father?" the first son asked.

"In the mornings I will hire men to work in the fields," he said. "It is then you shall go to the teacher. You will return home and work in the fields after mid-day."

Chung Yee looked at his mother to share her pleasure. He saw that she held her sleeve across her mouth and her black eyes sparkled.

Into the town, a water buffalo with a broken tether and a notched ear wandered up a narrow street to the teahouse. A young student looked at him and said:

"You must be the missing water buffalo of Ling Po that I have read about. Come with me, Old Fellow. You have caused enough trouble for one day."

The next morning from the house of Chung, six sons went to sit at the feet of the teacher in his garden of pomegranates and purple plums.

At noon, on the way home, they passed the rice field where Ling Po worked with his water buffalo.

Chung Yee heard the Old Farmer call out:

"Yi! You turnip. Another time, I shall tie you well. You will not get away soon again, Pig Headed One!"

Ahead of Chung Yee, his five brothers walked down the path in single file. Chung Yee was last, as he felt proper, since he was only the sixth son in the house of Chung.